PETERS

FRASER

&

D

*Chil***st**

WRITERS'   NTS

503
C
LO

D0297355

3 0 MAR 1994

Artwork by
Anthony Lewis

Y CANTER

A BANANA BOOK file copy.

Heather Maisner

ALICE'S MAGIC
ALICE BAND

Illustrated by
ANTHONY LEWIS

HEINEMANN · LONDON

William Heinemann Ltd
Michelin House
81 Fulham Road
London SW3 6RB

LONDON · MELBOURNE · AUCKLAND

First published 1992
Text © Heather Maisner 1992
Illustrations © Anthony Lewis 1992
ISBN 0 434 97680 6

Produced by Mandarin
Printed in Hong Kong

A school pack of BANANA BOOKS 49-54 is
available from Heinemann Educational Books
ISBN 0 435 00108 6

One, Two, Three, Four, Five

'IT'S A GIRL,' Alice's father said on the phone to his sister, Martha, in America. 'It's a girl and she looks like you.'

'Has she got any hair?' Aunt Martha asked, but the line was crackly and her voice was faint.

'Of course she'll have a high chair,' Alice's father said. 'But she was only born yesterday.'

'I said has she got any hair?' Martha shouted.

'Oh hair!' he replied. 'Yes, masses of it. And it's red like yours.'

'Great,' said Martha. 'I can't wait to see her.'

But Martha, who worked at a space research station and hardly ever took a holiday, didn't get to meet Alice until she was three.

On the day of Alice's third birthday
party, Aunt Martha swept into the room.
She wore a large straw hat and carried a
briefcase full of important papers covered
in sums, which she always took with her.
She scooped Alice into her arms and
kissed her.

'Look what I've got for you!' she said
and she drew from her briefcase, where it
lay sandwiched between the papers, a
green Alice band.

'I wore an Alice band like this all the
time when I was a child,' she said, and she
slipped the band over Alice's thick hair.

Then she loosened her own hair from
the hat she was wearing and it tumbled to

4

her waist, thick and red and wavy, just like
Alice's. Alice leapt into her arms and
kissed her.

'One, two, three, four, five,' she
whispered in Martha's ear.

'Alice can count,' Aunt Martha said.
'Say it again, Alice.'

Alice stared straight ahead, stroked her
Alice band and counted to one hundred.
Everybody was amazed. They all clapped.

Numbers Only

MARTHA STAYED A week. During that week Alice wore her Alice band all the time and she talked and talked. But she didn't tell stories or ask questions as other children did. Nor was she excited by the shapes and sounds of letters. She was only interested in numbers. When Martha returned to America, Alice continued to talk numbers.

By the time she was three and a half Alice could do all sorts of complicated adding-up. When she was four she could take-away, and at five she knew all the multiplication tables.

Whenever anyone came to tea, Alice invented games with numbers. She made her best friend Carly add up all the legs in the house, including the chairs and tables, the people and the pets. When Carly was tired of this game, Alice suggested they count each other's freckles instead. And Alice had a lot of freckles.

When Alice went for a walk with Ben next door, she invented games where they had to count the windows on the houses, take away the number of street lights and multiply by the number of cars parked in the road. When he muddled everything up, she laughed.

'Why can't we play hide-and-seek instead?' asked Ben.

'Because there aren't any sums in hide-and-seek,' Alice replied. 'And I only like playing games with sums.'

Alice always wore her Alice band. She wore it in the morning and at night, in the sunshine and the rain, in the sea and the swimming pool. She even wore it as she counted the soap bubbles in the bath.

Each morning as soon as Alice woke up, she felt her head for her Alice band. Then she counted her shoes, her socks and her books. She counted the animals on the curtains and the dots on the carpet, the stairs to the kitchen and the stripes on the hall wallpaper. She took away the number of birds in the garden and multiplied by the number of spoons on the table.

'She's just like you,' Alice's father wrote to Aunt Martha. 'She loves doing sums.'

School

THE DAY ALICE started school, she wore a green dress to match her green Alice band.

'Can anybody count to twenty?' the teacher asked.

Ben left out thirteen and Carly put nineteen and fourteen in the wrong places. Jimmy Jeffries said eleventeen instead of twenty. Amy Carter forgot about twelve, and Maria Gomez, who didn't speak any English, shook her head and wouldn't count at all. Alice said:

'I can count to one thousand.' And she
did. The children put up their hands and
called out that it was their turn now. But
Alice would not stop.

The next day Simon Lister said:

'Miss, I can count to one thousand too.'

'But do you know what ninety-one take away seventy-three makes?' Alice asked, and before he could work it out, she told him.

All that term Alice was better than anyone else at sums. Whenever the teacher asked a question, her hand went up, longer and straighter than anyone else's. If someone didn't know the answer, Alice shouted it out for them.

Simon Lister was good at sums too, but he didn't answer for anyone else. He helped them to work out the answers for themselves.

'Being good at sums isn't everything, you know,' Simon said. 'People learn by their mistakes.'

'But it's all too easy,' Alice replied. 'I don't see how everyone gets things so wrong.'

At playtime, when most children ran about, Alice sat alone doing sums. If Carly sat with her, Alice invented games where they had to count how many times Ben tripped over his own feet. Or how often Amy brushed her hair. And how many times Jimmy failed to score a goal.

But when Carly wanted her to play chase, Alice said:

'I don't want to. I want to play games with sums.'

Jimmy called out:

'Alice is scared all the numbers in her head will get muddled up if she runs.' And everybody laughed.

In class Carly often helped Alice with her spelling, but when Carly asked Alice to help her with her sums, Alice refused.

'I can't,' she said. 'I don't know how to help you and I don't know why. With sums you can either do them or you can't.'

Then even Carly didn't want to play with Alice any more.

The Tent

ONE HOT DAY in July, Alice's dad put up
a tent in the garden.

'Would you like to sleep in the tent?'
Alice asked Ben, who was peering over the
garden wall.

'No,' Ben said. 'I wouldn't.' For Ben, a

visit to Alice's house was worse than a visit to the dentist's. Sums were bad enough at school, where you had to do them. A night in a tent with Alice would be a night of mathematical agony. He jumped off the garden wall and ran indoors.

At school, Alice said to Carly:

'You'll come and sleep in my tent, won't you.'

'I can't,' Carly said. 'My mum wouldn't let me.' But Carly's mother was there, talking to Alice's mother, and Alice ran up to them.

'Please, please, please can Carly come and sleep in the tent?' she pleaded.

'Of course she can,' Carly's mother said, turning to her daughter. 'You'd love to sleep in a tent, wouldn't you dear?' Carly was upset. Alice had trapped her. She didn't want to go at all.

That evening, while Alice's mother prepared the supper, Alice invented more and more difficult sums for her friend.

'If there are seven peas in a pod and twenty pods, how many peas are there altogether?' she asked.

'If six people are coming to dinner and each person eats four and a half potatoes, how many potatoes have to be bought? And if each potato weighs twenty grams, what weight of potatoes will they need?'

By the time Carly lay down in the sleeping bag that night she was determined never to go to Alice's house again. It was hot and stuffy in the tent. Her head was spinning and, even as Alice fell asleep, she was *still* doing sums. Carly pulled the sleeping bag over her ears and fell into a fitful sleep. She dreamed that all the numbers, as large as trees, were marching towards her, chanting the

multiplication tables. The noise grew louder and louder. Carly woke up. It wasn't a dream; at least the chanting wasn't. A voice was saying the tables loud and clear. It was Alice.

'Six sixes are thirty-six. Seven sixes are forty-two. Eight sixes are forty-eight . . . '

Alice was stroking her Alice band and doing sums in her sleep! Carly was furious. She closed her eyes, but all she could hear was Alice's voice getting louder and louder. And she could see the numbers growing bigger and bigger.

Suddenly Carly rolled over towards Alice and snatched the Alice band from her head. Mid-way between seventy and seventy-seven, Alice sat up. Then she stopped chanting, closed her eyes and sank back onto the pillow. Soon she began to snore.

Carly tucked the Alice band into the
pocket of her school dress and fell asleep.

Where Oh Where Can My Alice Band Be?

'TIME TO GET up. Time to get up,'
Alice's mother called out. For the first
time ever, when Alice woke up, she didn't
immediately start counting everything
around her. The two girls washed and
dressed quickly.

'You aren't doing sums,' Carly said as
they ran to school.

'I don't want to do sums today,' said
Alice. 'I feel different.'

Half-way through the register, just as Miss Edwards came to her name, Alice realised why she felt different. Her hand went up in search of her Alice band, but it wasn't there.

'Alice Johnson?' Miss Edwards said. She was a new teacher and didn't know the children's names.

'My Alice band,' Alice cried out. 'My Alice band. Where's my Alice band?'

Miss Edwards peered down at the register.

'There isn't an Alice Band here,' she said. 'Only an Alice Johnson.'

'My Alice band has gone,' Alice wailed.

The class began to giggle.

'If Alice Band has gone,' Miss Edwards

said,' that explains why she isn't down in the register.'

The giggling grew louder.

'Please explain the joke,' Miss Edwards said. 'How many Alices are there in this class?'

'There's one Alice,' Ben said. 'Except there's usually kind of two.'

The whole class whooped with laughter and Miss Edwards began to look angry.

Simon Lister explained: 'The thing is, there's one Alice, but because she always wears an Alice band, that makes two.'

'Only today it's different,' Alice moaned. 'I've lost my Alice band and I don't feel like Alice at all. I can't think.'

'She's lost her band and she's thick as two planks,' screamed Sophie.

'She's falling apart. She's falling apart,' Jimmy Jeffries joked.

'Hurray! Her brains have disappeared. Now she's as stupid as the rest of us,' laughed Ben.

Miss Edwards told them to stop being silly and quieten down. But as lessons began, Alice wondered whether the things the children had said could be true. She sat very still and, whenever Miss Edwards seemed about to ask her a question, she looked the other way. At playtime Miss Edwards told Alice to go to

the sick room for a rest and she asked the
class to look for Alice's Alice band.

Out in the playground the boys and
girls ran off in all directions. They
crawled on hands and knees across the
lawn and squeezed between the bushes
and brambles along the school wall. Ben
began to climb the oak tree, which was out
of bounds and dangerous.

'I can see it,' he said. 'A bird must have picked it up then dropped it. It's caught in the top branches.'

The children gathered round and stared.

'I can't see anything,' Amy frowned.

'Because there isn't anything there,' said Carly. 'Get down, Ben. You'll fall.'

'But it's there,' Ben insisted. 'I know it is.'

'Well, I know it isn't,' said Carly. Everybody looked at her.

'How do you know?' Jimmy asked. 'How can you be so sure?'

'Because I know where it is.'

Carly hadn't meant to tell. She'd meant to slip the Alice band back into Alice's pocket, when Alice didn't expect it. But now with everyone waiting and watching, she felt she had to say something.

'You don't know,' Jimmy said. 'You don't know anything. You're a liar.'

'I'm not,' Carly cried. 'I do know where it is. It's here.' And she whisked the Alice band out of her pocket.

Fractions

'LET ME SEE,' said Jimmy.

He snatched the Alice band from Carly's hand and slipped it over his head. He stroked it with his hand and rolled his eyes as Alice usually did. Then he began:

'One six is six. Two sixes are twelve. Three sixes are eighteen . . . ' He recited the whole of the six times table, while the rest of the class pointed and giggled in amazement. Then Sophie said:

'Let me have a go.' She lifted the band from his head and slipped it over her own.

Immediately she began:

'One seven is seven. Two sevens are fourteen. Three sevens are twenty-one . . .'

Ben leapt down from the tree and yanked the band from Sophie's head and pulled it onto his own:

'Four sevens are twenty-eight. Five sevens are thirty-five. Six sevens are forty-two,' he said. Everyone cheered.

Ben had never been able to remember any of the tables before.

'So that's how Alice does it,' Simon said. 'She just strokes her Alice band and gets all the right answers.'

'Not any more,' said Jimmy. 'She's like the rest of us now. Maybe she's even more dumb.'

Ben reached the end of the seven times table and stood with a dazed, happy smile on his face.

'His head's in the clouds,' Sophie laughed.

'He's seven times better,' Jimmy joked.

'With an Alice band like this, who needs to study?' said Ben.

'Can I have a turn?' Maria asked. But Ben danced away.

'No,' he said. 'It's my band now. I'm going to keep it.'

'You can't,' cried Carly. 'Give it back to me. It's Alice's.'

'But I want a turn,' Maria said.

'So do I,' Amy cried, and she tried to grab hold of the band. Maria did too, but Ben held tight. The two girls pulled each end until the stitching came undone and the band snapped in half. Soon most of the class joined in, screaming and shouting:

'Give it to me. Give it to me.'

'There's only one thing for it,' Simon said and he ran back into the school.

'Where are you going?' Carly cried. 'What are you going to do?'

A few moments later he came back with a pair of scissors.

'Shut up or the teachers will come out,' he said.

Everyone stopped screaming and gathered round Simon. 'If we cut up the band, everyone will have some, won't

they?' he told them, as he carefully
snipped away and gave out the pieces.

'Here's yours,' he said, handing the last
piece to Carly, who took the tiny patch of
green material and burst into tears.

The bell sounded for the end of
playtime and the children filed back into
school. Miss Edwards said:

'Carly, would you like to tell Alice to
come back to class now, please.'

Only One Alice

CARLY PUSHED OPEN the sickroom
door. Alice sat with her head in her hands.

'You've got to come back now,' Carly
said.

'I can't without my Alice band,' Alice
said. 'Someone took it and I'll hate that
person for ever and ever.' She looked up
at Carly, her eyes wide and pleading.
'You're my only friend Carly, please help
me find it.'

'I'm not your friend,' Carly said. 'I'm the one you're going to hate for ever, because I'm the one who took your Alice band.'

Alice looked shocked. 'You mean you had it all the time?' she said.

'I'm sorry. I meant to give it back,' Carly replied, 'but now this is all I have.'

Carly told Alice what had happened in the playground and Alice sank back into the chair.

'What am I going to do?' she said. 'I've always worn my Alice band. I can't think without it. I'll keep making mistakes and everyone will laugh at me.'

'You won't make any more mistakes than anyone else,' said Carly. 'And nobody will laugh at you. They'll probably like you more.'

'I'll never be able to get the right answers again.'

'Of course you will. Just because you haven't got your Alice band, it doesn't mean you're stupid. You can do anything you want if you try.'

Back in the classroom, Alice sat quietly at her desk with her head lowered. Miss Edwards asked:

'Who would like to run through the six times table?'

Several children put up their hands and she asked Sophie to begin. Sophie placed a piece of green material on her head and said very confidently:

'One six is six. Two sixes are twelve. Three sixes are eighteen . . . '

'Please, Miss, ask me,' Ben interrupted. He stood up, placed some green material on his head and continued:

'Four sixes are twenty-four. Five sixes are thirty. Six sixes are thirty-six . . . '

Then Amy took over. And so it went on right through the six, seven and eight times tables. All the children, even the ones who hadn't known them the day before, knew their tables today. Miss Edwards wasn't too sure about the green material, but the results were excellent.

'Well done class,' she said. 'What a splendid team you make. Now, Alice, perhaps you'd like to run through the nine times table for us?'

Alice stood up and her hand automatically reached up for her Alice band. When it wasn't there, she shook her head and began to sit down again.

'Her brains have slipped,' Ben laughed.

'Ask me, Miss. Ask me,' called Sophie, but Miss Edwards waited for Alice.

Carly squeezed Alice's hand under the desk.

'Come on. You can do it,' she whispered. 'You know you can.'

Everyone turned to look at Alice.

'Er . . . I'm not sure . . . Er . . . I think . . . Um . . . One nine is nine,' she began. 'Er . . . two nines are eighteen. Three nines are is . . . er . . . twenty-five. No. Er. Twenty-seven. Four nines are thirty-eight. I mean thirty-six. Five nines are forty-five. Six nines are fifty-four . . . '

From then on Alice managed to recite

the whole of the nine times table without a mistake. Everyone looked surprised. They even began to clap. Alice flopped back into her seat.

'I knew you could do it,' Carly said. 'You can do sums just like before.'

Simon leant across. 'I'm sorry about the Alice band,' he said. 'We shouldn't have done it. If we give you back the pieces, maybe you can sew them together again.'

'It's all right. It was only an old Alice band,' said Alice. 'Who needs an Alice band?' A smile spread across her face. 'If an Alice band is cut up into twenty-four pieces and shared between a class of twelve children, how many pieces will each child get?'

Everybody groaned.